JILLY'S
Terrible Temper Tantrums
~ AND ~
How She Outgrew Them

written by Martha Heineman Pieper, Ph.D.

illustrated by Jo Gershman

DEDICATIONS

In memory of William J. Pieper ~ M.H.P.

For Andy, Gabriel, and Riley ~ J.G.

ACKNOWLEDGEMENTS

Great gratitude to first readers Rebecca Baldwin, Elizabeth Hersh, Kelly Perez, Victoria Pieper, Gershon Pieper, and Tamara Sitkoff for their invaluable input. M.H.P.

SMART L♥VE PRESS

Jilly's Terrible Temper Tantrums: And How She Outgrew Them
by Martha Heineman Pieper, Ph.D.
Text copyright 2016 by Smart Love Press, LLC.
Illustrations copyright 2016 by Jo Gershman.

For permissions write:
Smart Love Press, LLC
400 E. Randolph Street, Suite 1905
Chicago, IL 60601

Book design and cover design by Jo Gershman.
Illustrations rendered in watercolor & colored pencil.

Summary: When Jilly, a happy little kangaroo, has a series of Terrible Temper Tantrums, her parents lovingly help her through them. Children will be very familiar with the frustrations that trigger Jilly's upset feelings, and will applaud her dawning understanding that seeking help and a hug is far superior to the misery of a temper tantrum.

Library of Congress Control Number: 2016917348
ISBN: 978-0-9838664-1-1 (library binding)
First Edition: 2017
10 9 8 7 6 5 4 3 2

[1.Temper tantrums-Juvenile fiction. 2.Parenting-Juvenile fiction.
3.Discipline-Juvenile fiction. 4.Animal Stories-Juvenile fiction.]

WEBSITES
www.smartlovepress.com
www.jillysterribletempertantrums.com

printed in the United States

Ages three and up.

Jilly was a happy little kangaroo who loved to play with her big brother, Joey, listen to stories, give and get hugs and cuddles, and have tea parties with her stuffed animals.

But once in a while . . . .

Jilly had

a

Terrible **T**emper **T**antrum.

I want to play too!

"I'm sorry, Jilly," said Father. "But only two of us can play chess at a time. I would love to play with you when the game is over. Can you build a tower or draw a picture while you wait?"

"No! NO! NO! Play with me NOW!
I hate waiting!"
And up, up, up she hopped.
And down, down,

d o w n

she came,

splat

in the middle of the chessboard!

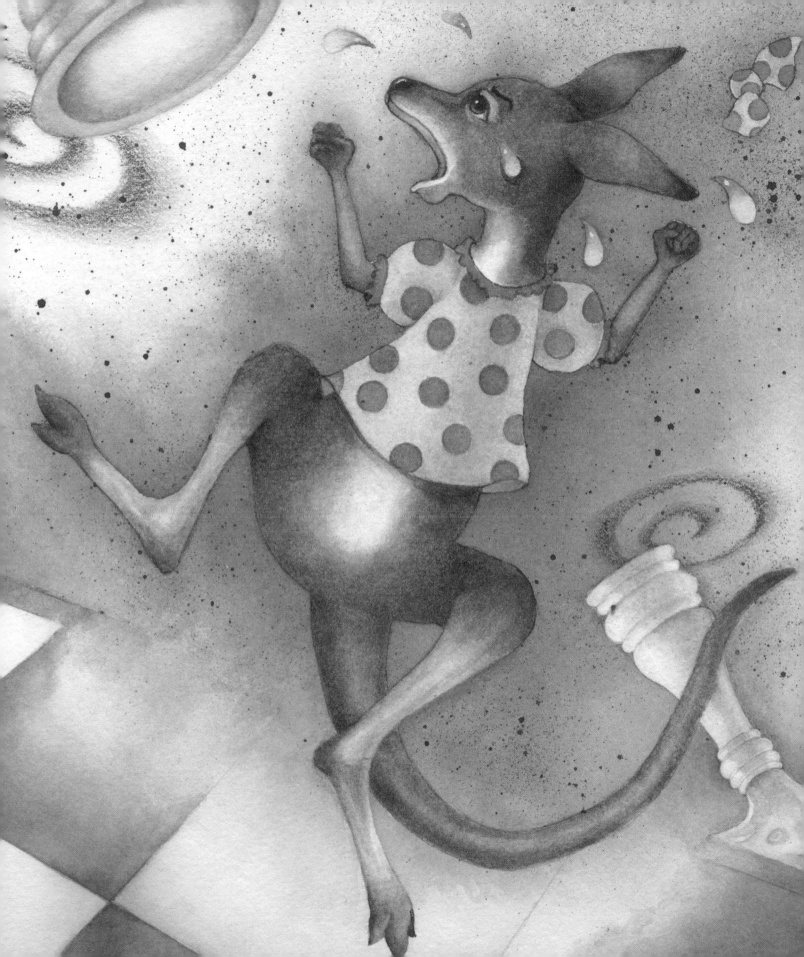

"Oh, Jilly, I know it's hard to wait," said Father, "but turning over the board just makes the game longer, and being so upset is NO fun. Is there something else you would like to do while we play? And when the chess game is over, we can read a story or have a tea party."

NO! NO! NO! NOW! NOW! NOW!

"Jilly, wouldn't you rather cuddle with me than feel so unhappy?

I'm always here for a snuggle,
even if I can't play with you
at the moment."

And soon, Jilly was a happy little kangaroo once more.

a few weeks later

Edith Echidna came over to play
and Jilly had
another
Terrible **T**emper **T**antrum.

"Let's play hopping games!" said Jilly.
"How about hopscotch?"
"No," said Edith.
"I want to play hide-and-seek."

And she curled up into a ball
and rolled off to hide
before Jilly could say a word.

"It's hard when a friend comes over and doesn't want to play what you want to play," said Mother. "Can I help? How about a hug?"

"NO!" cried Jilly. "She won't do what I want. **I don't like her anymore!**"

"Hop with me, Jilly. You might feel better if we look for Edith and talk with her about taking turns choosing games. I would be happy to help you find her."

Jilly sniffed. "Okay."

"We found you, Edith!" shouted Jilly.

"Yes," said Mother, "and now that you two have played hide-and-seek, why don't you play a hopping game?"

And soon, Jilly was a happy little kangaroo once more.

a few weeks later

Jilly had
another
Terrible **T**emper **T**antrum.

·ENTER·

·TOY STORE·

"Jilly dear," said Mother, "which toy would you like to choose today?"

"I want TWO toys," said Jilly.

"I know, sweetheart. With so many toys here, it is difficult to pick just one, but do you remember we said one toy today? Which one is your favorite?"

"It's disappointing when you can't have as many toys as you want," said Mother, "but being so upset is making you feel worse. Let's think about which toy you would like today, and which one you would like to get next time."

I want two!
I want
TWO!

Father gently
picked Jilly up
and hopped with her
for a while . . . .

"Tell me," said Father,
"which one would you like
to take home today?"
"This one," sobbed Jilly.
"Great!" said Father.
"Can you give the other
toy back? The sales clerk
will keep it until the
next time we come."

And soon, Jilly was a happy little kangaroo once more.

Jilly started to have
another
Terrible **T**emper **T**antrum.

"Oh no, not again!
Stay **UP**!"

"I'm mad!

I need a hug!

I need Mama!"

"I need a hug!" cried Jilly.
"My tower keeps falling down when
I want it to stay up and be tall.
It's making me MAD!
Will you help me?"

"I am so proud of you, Jilly,
for telling me what is wrong
and asking for help.
Good job!"

And soon, Jilly was a VERY happy little kangaroo once more.

AUTHOR'S NOTE

Jilly's parents have adopted the Smart Love® approach to managing children's behavior, which I call Loving Regulation. Loving Regulation avoids both the negativity of discipline and the laxity of permissiveness by regulating children's behavior in a firm but loving manner. It avoids the pitfalls of either giving in to tantrums or imposing sanctions, such as time-outs or consequences. Permissiveness prevents children from learning to regulate themselves, while traditional forms of discipline are harmful because they teach children to be harsh toward themselves and toward others with whom they disagree.

In contrast, children guided by Loving Regulation learn that, while they may have to give up a desired gratification, they need never lose the affection and closeness of the parent-child relationship. In fact, like Jilly, children will discover that true happiness comes not from the gratification of any particular desire, but from making constructive choices within a relationship of ongoing warmth with parents or other caregivers. Equally important, children will imitate the Loving Regulation they receive and grow into tolerant adults who can respond compassionately and without anger to differences of opinion with others – a quality both individuals and the modern world surely and sorely need.

If you are interested in learning more about Loving Regulation and the Smart Love approach, see *Smart Love: The Comprehensive Guide to Understanding, Regulating, and Enjoying Your Child.*